# Uncle Al's Perverse, Gay and Kink Verse

# Uncle Al's Perverse, Gay and Kink Verse

## Al Smith

iUniverse, Inc.
Bloomington

# Uncle Al's Perverse, Gay and Kink Verse

iUniverse books may be ordered through booksellers or by contacting:

iUniverse
1663 Liberty Drive
Bloomington, IN 47403
www.iuniverse.com
1-800-Authors (1-800-288-4677)

ISBN: 978-1-4620-4047-6 (sc)
ISBN: 978-1-4620-4048-3 (ebk)

Printed in the United States of America

iUniverse rev. date: 08/04/2011

# Concise Advice
29 December 2010

If you think morals have descended
Are up tight or easily offended,
Put down this ridiculous book
And give something else a look.
This isn't your kind of reading,
The writing reflects ill-breeding.

# Our Power
19 November 2010

We have the Bill of Rights and reason,
Not trite laws that make every act treason.

I

Tho everybody's glad it there and it's thorny like a
cactus,
Congress shall make no law regulating religious
practice.
Congress shall make no law abridging the freedom of
speech.
Personal expression's within everyone's reach.
The government may not exert dominion
Over freedom of the press or opinion.
The government may not violate
The right of the people to congregate.
The People have a right to redress
Against any governmental excess.

II

This thought make liberals comes unhinged,
The right of the people to keep and bear arms shall
not be infringed.

III

No Soldier shall, in time of peace abide
In any house without the owner allied.

### IV

Whether participating in business or leisure
People have a right against unreasonable search and
seizure.
No Warrant shall issue but upon probable cause
Supported by oath or affirmation that draws
A description of the place to be sought
And the persons or things to be brought.

### V

No person shall be subject for the same offense
Twice, nor a witness against self-defense,
Nor be be deprived of life, liberty or property
Without due process of law and formality.

### VI

In all criminal prosecutions, regardless of style,
The accused shall enjoy the right to a speedy trial,
By an impartial jury to be convicted or acquitted
Of the district wherein the crime shall have been
committed;
And to be informed of the nature and cause of the
informing against,
To be confronted with bthe witnesses conforming
against;
To have compulsory process for obtaining witnesses
in his favor,
And to have the assistance of counsel to act as his saver.

### VII

In Suits at common law, trial by jury shall not be thinned
And no fact tried by a jury shall be otherwise
re-examined.

## VIII
Excessive bail shall not be required or afflicted
Nor excessive fines imposed, nor cruel punishments inflicted.

## IX
The enumeration of certain rights shall not be construed
To deny or disparage others retained by the multitude.

## X
The powers not delegated to the United States administration
Are reserved to the States or the people of the nation.

Reasons for the constitution are annihilated
When the rights of the people are violated.

*This isn't vulgar or pornographic, but it'll corrupt your mind forever.*

# Eye Pled Alley
3 Feb 2011

Eye pled alley gents tooth a flagon the unit estates ovum Erika and to their public four witches' tans, won Asian underdog, invisible with libber tea and just ice for all.

I'm not sure what it means, but I think it talks about free iced tea.

I pledge allegiance to the Constitution of The United States of America and to the principles for which it stands, one nation of many states with liberty and justice for all.

# 90 Second Leather Speech

for 2010 Mr. San Diego Leather contest

In a life full of stories
My earliest memories
Go back to Sunday School
And learning the golden rule.
The kids with me then
Were still in the same pool
Several years later when
We graduated from high school.
The last time I went to a class reunion
I felt we had nothing in common
I had a strong sense of disunion.
I only wanted to run.
That's a sharp contrast
To when I'm with leather folk.
With you I never feel outcast
And that's no joke.
You are my people, my tribe.
It's hard for me to describe,
My feelings run deep inside.
Regardless of any personal difference
I challenge you to pursue excellence
Becoming a person of quality
Living life with a touch of frivolity.

# Balm of My Palm

22 July 2010

I'm salivating tired of waiting
While contemplating and anticipating
Activating, propagating,
And proliferating masturbating.

Yes, I'm advocating, articulating
Communicating and motivating
The accommodating, collaborating
And participating in masturbating.

Anything facilitating, orchestrating,
Adulating, commemorating,
Congratulating, demonstrating,
Or relating to masturbating

I find invigorating, elating
And liberating, creating
Jubilating, celebrating
And venerating of masturbating.

# Bawdy Body

6 March 2010

Kiss me from my eye to my thigh.
Blow on me from my ear to my rear.
Lick me from my gut to my butt.
Touch me from my lip to my hip.
Taste the forbidden fruit.
Play with my root
Chakra. Explore more
Of what we're here for.
Without hesitation
Let romance
And sensation
Begin to enhance
The erotic stimulation.
Let's remeasure
Our level of pleasure.
Let our interaction
Start a chain reaction.
Take me over the top,
More, more, don't stop.
My body's all yours
And I'm out of metaphors.
I really don't mind
If you help me find
The splendid sights
From obscene heights.
The universe's within reach
As I let out a screech
A tidal wave of sensation
Culminates the mobilization
Of intercourse and interaction
To mutual satisfaction.

From this time hence
There is no sense
In trying to compare
A feeling that rare.
Filed forever in my memories
Are the rockets and glories
Of your bestowment
Of that special moment.
I don't care if they call it a sin,
I just want to do it again.

*Al O spoke and Al S wrote*

# Bear Dare
25 July 2010

I don't care if my belly shows,
I'm dancing with very little clothes.
The go-go boy is chancing
Cruising for a bruising.
It's the box on which I'm dancing,
He can have when I'm thru using.

# Beyond Abscond
14 November 2010

The Hard Edge
Deconstructing Privilege
How sick and twisted can you be?
I invite you to go there with me.
Yo, crazy messed up psycho bitch
Come over here and scratch my itch.
This is the real thing and we're not going to sim it.
We're going to push each other to the limit.
Find what's authentic
And makes us tick
Without being apologetic
Sense it to the core
To get a lot more
Of what we're here for
Each on a personal journey
Overcoming the tyranny
That for our well being
And was bred into us
By society that was well-meaning
But misled, of course.
It served as a way to survive
Now we're learning how to thrive
And feel fully alive.
Who can be coerced
Into going first?
I tell you no stories or lies
Respect my boots and nobody dies.

I need to take the words you're said
And run them thru my head.
I thought, "What the heck?"
When you put your hands around my neck.
I'm going to poke needles in your hide,
Then I'll smack them till you bleed inside.
To a certain extent
We want to vent
While society does its best to prevent
The occurrence of such an event.
Afterward feeling emotionally spent
But feeling freeing
To the fiber of my being
Not just trying
But really flying
Out past the sky
On an endorphin high
An existential brush
From an endorphin rush.
Oh yeah, this is where I belong!
Why the hell did I wait so long?

# Indulges and Bulges
24 June 2010

Walking down the street I ogle and stare
At Dore Alley and Folsom Street Fair.
The men are more than just pretty faces,
They have muscles and bulges in the right places.
Any one of them can sign up on my dance card
Just looking at them makes me drool and get hard.
Their looks and bodies are hard to hide
Especially when they're naked outside.
The entry signs say no fucking or nudity
But those in the know don't put up with such prudity.
As San Francisco's finest reposed
I've strolled by with my privates exposed.
Regardless of the weather
Most of the crowd wears leather.
There are people of both sexes and all sizes
And a few come with odd surprises.
I get my favorite wish there
To walk around in fetish gear.
When the sky's unclouded
The street becomes crowded.
You never know who you'll meet,
And you might have sex in the street.
Folsom & Dore are a mix of fantasy and real
Mostly you just look, but sometimes you feel.
There's drooling by the hour
With no hope of a cold shower.

Later when the fog rolls in,
It's the rigamarole's end.
Outside the temperature drops
But indoors the party never stops.
The memories are all so good
I'll be back next time in all likelihood.

# Care To Wear

6 September 2010

There were no mishaps,
I dressed in boot and chaps.
That's all the clothing I wore,
Boots, chaps and nothing more.
I didn't dress that way to tease,
It made me comfortable, at ease.
It was fine for reading email,
But if I went outside, I risked jail.
A troubling dilemma arose
When it came time to put on clothes.
What can I wear that's comfortable for me
And still passes muster in society?

addendum by Rusty Mills

The answer will always depend
On the location where you end.
In San Francisco, chaps and boots
Are more popular than business suits.
Letting people see your butt
Dick, boobs or cunt is what
Gets you cheers and hugs,
And sometimes strokes and tugs.
I'm going to go out naked there
And show my hard dick everywhere.

# Stoked by Being Poked

4 March 2011

The sting was slight
Like a mosquito bite.
My skin had been swabbed clean
For a temporary piercing scene.
At this time, at this stage
The needles were small gauge.
Then came another pinch
That didn't make me flinch.
The needle was true
As it went straight thru.
My piercer began to reckon
It was time to check in.
I was able joke and converse
And the pain wasn't getting worse.
I was more than ready,
My breathing was steady.
Then came an additional prick
From another needle stick.
"So the scene can continue
In spite of the needles in you?"
A couple more got put in
Just under the skin.
The occasion was more merry
Than gross or scary.
Lesson learned behooved
The needles be removed.
The pain was less without a doubt
Of the needles pulling out.

With the needle acquittal
I bled just a little.
With a gentle rub and swipe
It was cleaned with an alcohol wipe.
I got high without any drug
And we separated with a hug.

# Circumcision Decision

6 Sept 2010

Parents need to understand there's no obligation
To subject their boys to genital mutilation.
The result is lifetime mental scarification.
It's time to stop this circumcision abomination
And get over denial of harm by the whole nation.

# Connecting the Dots
19 August 2010

I think I have been underestimating the power of sex. Let's consider the holy trinity of love, sex and marriage. Because I'm gay until recently I only focused on putting love & marriage together. Anybody familiar with the way gay men act, knows that in the gay community frequently sex has nothing to do with emotions or commitment. Sex between men is a simple act of pleasure for pleasure's sake. That's where conservatives get their panties in a knot. Sex between a man and a woman takes negotiation, give a little to get a little. There's the rub. Gays get lots of free and easy sex while for straight men it comes at a price.

The other day at work in the lunchroom I saw an older coworker holding hands with her husband. From past observations I know the woman is very religious. Then it hit me. She gets to have church and sex together. As an excommunicated gay man I had never connected religion and erotic that way before. The thought of sex with a woman doesn't do anything for me, but the message I get from larger society is that sex with a woman feels very good. Now if you combined the emotional high of religious ecstasy with sexual ecstasy, you just couldn't get any higher than that. Marriage frequently is a religious rite. Which puts sex under the church umbrella. Then after marriage, all societal messages and blessings are saying go for the gusto. In my life never having connected church and sex, I think I've been cheated.

Now let's expand the religion-sex connection a bit. The way I understand it, suicide bombers make the sacrifice on the promise of sex in the afterlife. After all, what's the point of having 72 virgins if you don't get to deflower them? In Mormon theology, people are eventually resurrected with fully functioning bodies. And the faithful ones benefiting from Heavenly Father's presence go on to become like Him, as gods themselves peopling other worlds with their own spirit children. Now just how do you suppose those spirit children come about? Could it be sex? In other words, obedient Mormon men get to have sex forever; and not all with the same wife.

Maybe the way I connected love and marriage without sex can be twisted to an analogy of why straight men oppose gay marriage. Straight men, the power brokers in today's world, having connected marriage and sex, are repulsed by the thought of marriage being represented by two men having sex. And don't mention polyamory. They aren't even going there. Maybe polygamy, but not polyamory.

Yes, I think I've been underestimating the power of sex. Life experience leads me to conclude that decisions are made emotionally then rationalized logically. Because some people can't conceive of themselves in a same-gender marriage or polyamorous arrangement, they seek to deny those relationships to all others.

# Survey of the Day
31 March 2011

The surprise poll for the day
Is a short porn survey.
A new adult business
Is looking to reduce stress
By finding out what others want,
What to film, sell and flaunt.
The movies will be beyond bawdy
Showing favorite parts of the body.
Do you like your men to play roles,
How about featuring glory holes?
What about naughty S&M boys
Playing with each other & their toys?
What if we mix girls and guys,
How do you feel about bi's.
As you watch are you hopin'
For public sex out in the open?
As we try to please all sorts,
Should we focus on water sports?
Do you want scenes to be light and flirty
Or just jump right into down and dirty?
What about body and facial hair,
A twink, a chub or a bear?
Do you fantasize about sex in cars,
How about smoking cigarettes or cigars?
Do you like men who are cowboys or truckers,
Or when naked, do they look like the same fuckers?
Does it matter where the scene takes place,
Or if the participants are of a different race?
Of course the promo and hype
Will feature the perfect body type.

# Dyed~In~The~Wool Incompatible
7 January 2011

For believers, God is the source,
A happiness and goodness resource.
When atheists avow
"No god in my life now.
I behave as I should.
I'm happy and life is good."
This declaration flies in faith's face
And they have to put humanists in their place
By framing them as bitter and nihilistic,
Which comes across as patently unrealistic.
The evidence is God doesn't control the universe,
But that view is rejected and deemed perverse.

# Folsom Pablum
## 29 Sept 2010

With limp wrist bones
Not flaunting rhinestones
Touching cheekbones
Not acting like clones
But talking on cell phones
With innuendo overtones
Influenced by pheromones
And driven by hormones
Like androsterone
And testosterone
With anatomy everybody owns
Showing off on curbstones
Ignoring chaperones
Modesty unthrones
Going for end zones
Evoking groans & moans
Like jazz saxophones
Reaching erotic milestones

# Gathering Blathering

30 July 2010

Come whoever you are
Worshiper of solitude,
Come from near and far
You who exude attitude.
Mundanes don't understand
There's not many like us
Scattered throughout the land.
Gathering is a great impetus,
A chance to be with our kind,
People with similar taste,
Mingle with others of like mind
And forget about the straitlaced.
Let's celebrate our making,
Dancing naked in the sunlight
Worries we'll be forsaking
While setting the world right.

# I Hesitate, Then No Date

31 March 2011

When I see his handsome face
My timid heart starts to race,
But a date isn't going to take place
Because I can't get to first base..

The obstacle to cheap thrills
Is my lack of social skills.
Unlike other aches or ills
There isn't a cure by pills.

I try to converse, laugh and negotiate
But I don't speak my mind until it's too late
And the subject is closed without debate,
So I end up going home to masturbate.

# Hymn to SM
24 December 2010

At the Church of Body and Spirit
Christmas Eve we got to do and hear it.
Religious fanatics are right about one goal
Mortification of the flesh can lead to growth of the
soul.
At least the boundaries of separation are overcome
By pushing the limits of sensation outcome.
It's quite easy to evoke pain
So we put the body under strain
For the byproduct of endorphin
Going to the max again and again.
Beyond too much and over the top
Is where we go and then stop.
Mainstream says it's perverted and a sin,
But from the way we feel, we'll do it again.

# Met on the Internet

31 October 2010

Although in life we've never met
I saw your face on the internet.
My heart was caught by surprise
By the look in your eyes.
While reading your profile
I just had to smile.
I was going to contact you for a date
Then I realized really you're straight.

*I wrote this to an acquaintance who is gay but stays married to a woman.*

# Ought Thought

29 January 2010

Dude, dude, what can I say
So you won't take this the wrong way?
GET OVER YOURSELF!
Take your life off the shelf.
In your head is all this clamor.
You're hitting your head with a hammer.
To me it's pretty plain
You're in great pain.
Your life has gone stale.
It's vigor is beginning to fail.
You're weakening, about to drop,
You're asking if you should stop.
So far you've avoided the big one
But by small pains you're undone.
Bite the bullet,
Make the split,
Cut out the bullshit.
Eventually by and by
Everyone recognizes the lie.
Staying is not fair to both.
It stunts your growth.
What I say is not for my gain.
Only you can end your own pain.

Dude, dude, what do you want me to say,
"Play kissy face" and "Have a nice day?"
You're on your knees
Praying for guarantees.
Life is unsure, uncertain
And no one knows about that final curtain.
I've told you before
And here it is once more,
End the internal strife
And get an authentic life!
"My, my what shall I do?
There's a pebble in my shoe.
If I remove it the pain will go away
But another one will come to stay."
Pain is the body's way of saying
Attention you're not paying.
Removing long-term trouble
May reveal unaddressed rubble.
I hope my words don't offend.
I want to be your friend.
This poem may be banal,
But I'm always yours, Al.

# Conversations, Rations and Celebrations

5 May 2011

I went to my friends' for pizza night,
Looking forward to that weekly delight.
I dressed with the kilt-and-no-shirt look.
Other friends were there with foresight,
They brought mixed fruit and a book
About Lucrecia, the daughter of a crook.
After being married against her will
She started to write her own guidebook.
Her beginning battles were all uphill.
The tales of her deeds give us a thrill.
She became a master of misdirection.
It was like she had a license to kill.
Pizza was baked and came as a selection
One a green pepper and mushroom confection,
The other was pepperoni and Parmesan;
All blending for a friendship connection.
Then we sang "Happy Birthday" to John
And he blew out the candles with aplomb.
The chocolate cake was put to good use.
Next it was time for some to move on,
The book couple decided to vamoose,
But three others came to introduce
A different party atmosphere.
Their actions were fast and loose
Coming down the stair
Dressed in underwear
They touched and kissed
Acting brazen like on a dare,
As if their purpose to exist
Was to spend their time blissed.

The hot tub had been heating
And that was hard to resist.
Clothing removal was fleeting
And there was plenty of seating.
The horseplay continued
Slowly we started overheating
Not to be misconstrued
Stroking was viewed
In an appreciative light
And hanky-panky ensued.

# Scenes of Jeans
24 June 2010

By all ways and means
Give me a man in jeans,
Wearing the worn and torn kind
That show off a little behind.
Where the cloth has worn thin
Let me look and see skin.
It makes me drool and smile
When a man goes commando style.
Not every guy has the gall
To flaunt custom and freeball.
Not to be too blunt
But I like holes in front.
It really gets me going
When your cock is showing.
Holes are an attention getter
And the more the better.
Let me see the hot rocket
You've got in your pocket.
Yes, wear jeans faded and worn
With holes that are ripped and torn.
I don't care if they're trashed or mesh
Just as long as you flash some flesh.

My intent diverts and vision distorts
When I see a man in short shorts.
Lift your legs in the air
Without any underwear,
Giving me an unobstructed view
To prove you're a man thru and thru.

# Sex Vortex

13 June 2010

Following extended foreplay
The way we acted was insane,
We started banging away
Like a screen door in a hurricane.
Before long I shot my load
And let the world know as I came
Screaming until we slowed,
Just adding glory to my fame.

# Ripped and Stripped
11 February 2011

I want a man with hair,
Give me a cub or bear,
Not just furry but hustle up
And rustle some muscle up.
Give me a grubstake
On a piece of beefcake.

I'll watch like a glutton
As he starts to unbutton
His shirt to reveal
A chest of steel
With pierced nipples
Above ab ripples.
I'm such a slut
To drool over his gut.
Turning his broad back
Gives my lust no slack.
Gradually he drops his jeans
Then slowly he bends and leans
Over to pull off his pants
Giving me a chance glance
Of his buttocks and hole,
Then turning, I see his pole.
Stretching and acting unafraid
He showcases a form manmade.
There he stands in full glory
And that's the end of my story.

# Station Variation
August 2009

## Impact
Make a fist and hit
It may hurt a bit
Pound & punch away
Can you take it all day?
Is it your wish
To take all I dish?

## Electricity
Let me give you a jolt
It won't be a thunderbolt
We'll start with just a tingle
And ramp up the juice 'til you jingle
Ping, ping, ping, ping
Until you sing.

## CBT
Let me give you a tap
I'll keep it consistent
Like a soft slap
Soon the insistent
Vibrations of rap, rap
Will send sensations
Of nerve modulations

**Flogging**
Just look at the cat of nine tails
The very picture of prison & jails
As it hits my back
Give me no slack
Put me in my place
Send me into alternate space.

**Single Tail**
Oh the whip long
Single tail so strong
Such a quick sting
You make me sing
I raise my voice
To my toy of choice.

**Waxing**
Go on by the hour,
Please don't stop.
Give me a hot shower
Of wax drop by drop.
Yes, the hot wax
Helps me relax.

**Spanking**
I'll be the slut.
You get out the planking.
I'll put out my butt,
You give me a spanking.
I really mean thanks
For all the spanks.

## Caning
To begin the skin
Is not virgin.
Don't you constrain;
What keeps me sane
I attain from the pain
Of a cane.

## Fisting
I'll make a fist
That's hard to resist
And insert it to my wrist.
Then with a twist
I'll be assisting
Your liking of fisting.

## Fusion
It's all about sensation
And intense stimulation.
This is my ode
To sensory overload.
Let the endorphins flow.
Bring on that afterglow.

# Stray Play
3 October 2010

Sorry my response is late,
It took time to create
Something pleasing and laudatory
From our adventuresome story.

It was my honor to bequeath
A SM scene on Keith.
In the bar we talked
And shared more as we walked
A short space
To his place.
His living quarters were spare
And we made do with what was there.
Keith wanted to be restrained
And his movements refrained,
So with cords he was bound
To keep from moving around.
From a bit of inspiration
To increase the sensation
I thought it would be cool
To use my multi-purpose tool.
Using the dull side of the blade,
I faked the cuts I made.
But the sensation was real enough
Keith thought we were playing tough.

It didn't disappoint
When I used the tool point
Pressed into his tit
And stimulated him to emit
Cum, that wonderful slime.
Then unfortunately it was time
I was getting really tired
And an exit was required.
We took a few minutes to huddle
While we did a quick cuddle.
After we adjourned I learned
My tool didn't get returned.
I'll be in Keith's possession
Until the next occasion.
So Keith played with a poet
And didn't know it.

# Lewd Attitude

15 May 2011

Okay, I'll admit my addiction
At an event of healthy friction
Also called wanking or masturbation
Attended by men from around the nation
Indulging in manual manipulation.
Touching what feels good
Sensing as it should,
Showing genitals bare
Turning software into firmware.
Doing what comes naturally,
Stroking freely and easily.
I'm sure you understand
We took matters in hand.
Some men enjoyed watching DVDs
Making their cocks as big as you please
With porn stars so hunky,
Spanking the monkey,
Choking the chicken
Feeling the penis thicken.
Truly a time to diddle
Each man with his fiddle,
Playing the flute tool,
Distracted by pocket pool,
A visit by Rosy Palm and her five daughters
While fantasizing about cubs, bears or otters.
Practicing autoeroticism,
Perfecting Onanism,
Lube the love pump,
Make the slug jump,

Beat your meat,
Flog your log,
Hold your sausage hostage,
Jerkin' the gherkin,
Tussle with your muscle,
Hone the bone,
Wank the crank,
Pump the stump.
Jerk off, jack off,
Wank off, whack off,
Play with yourself,
Pleasure yourself,
Touch yourself,
Self-gratification,
Self-manipulation,
Self-service,
Self-pollution,
No-date solution.
Bash the bishop,
Man to hand relationship,
Polish your knob,
Butter corn on the cob,
Squeeze the tomato,
Smash the potato.
Do you share it
When you peel your carrot?
Pet the cat, pat the brat
Hand to man combat.
Stay on the wagon
And drain the dragon.

Generate sperm
And burp the worm.
Most liked waiting and hedging
So participated in edging
Putting off and delaying the climax
Until they could push it to the max.
It was a sensory celebration
With men of like inclination.
I left with memory souvenirs
To fuel fantasies for years.

# Party Hearty
27 April 2011

I was excited to get
An email to the birthday
And dawg party for Brett.
The event was under way
When I arrived, the door was ajar,
I left my card with more of the same
Dropped by others on the side bar.
And in a short time frame
I excused myself to pass thru
The few chatting in the kitchen
And stepped down into
The backyard where more men
Were drinking and socializing.
Where I ran into a couple of friends
Who I greeted by vocalizing
About recent life trends.
Roy still paints a little
Tho teaching keeps him occupied.
Mike was noncommittal
About his blog being modified.
I left to mix and mingle
To see who else I knew
Acting like I was single
And find a partier, too.
Down a short side alley
The distant light beckoned
To Brett's workshop galley
With animal masks, I reckoned.

Then it was time to lunge in
Shirtless, chest bared
To the play dungeon
For those who dared.
I was able to connect
And knelt down for sucking
With a man who was erect
That lead to bareback fucking.
Making noises and fooling around
Entertaining ourselves and other men,
Going at it for another round,
There was more sucking again.
Proving men are pigs
Going for sexual stimulation
When there are no prigs
Who object to masturbation.
The firepit's radiant heat
Felt good on bare skin
An outside retreat
For conversation sharin'.
Enjoyed by each to his taste,
A party like others before
To interact without haste
Hoping next time for more.

# Beat and Greet
2 May 2011

The event was called Beat and Great,
A chance for like minds to meet,
Held at a private location,
A secret destination.
The door on its conforming hide
Gave no clue about what was inside.
We got past the doorpost
By signing papers with the host.
As evil sadistic paradises
Go, it was filled with devices.
Papa Tony was demagogging
Giving a 101 on flogging.
In the corner we started an adorement
Of discomfort by tit torment.
Sensation was ramped up
By tits being clamped up.
Curious onlookers came by
And a few gave it a try.
Pinch, twist and then pull
To give torture in full.
His contorted facial expressions
Told me how to pace the sessions.
A post-event email, sent with latitude
Was laudatory and filled with gratitude.

# Man Stan

26 June 2011

Master, Master Stan,
He's the man,
He can do it, sure he can.

As you explore your role
Of Master from your soul,
I encourage time spent hence
With a sub or slave together
Learning conjointly since
You're journeying into leather.

# Meditation Exploration
5 July 2011

I went out to salute the day.
Sunshine saturated my bare skin.
The breeze caressed my body's display.
In addition to the sun's kissin',
I touched myself erotically.
My erection stood out pulsating
Enjoying the sun asymptotically.
Casually I sat down, situating
My root chakra against Mother Earth.
Connected to nature, masturbating
To the point of orgasm, giving birth
To the sensation of completeness.
In the lull of repose I had a largess
Of inspiration, ending the process.

# Yen of Men

13 November 2010

Driving away the day's aggravation,
Hoping for a little affirmation,
Praying for no disappointment,
No fly in the ointment,
With a look of lust
He stared at her bust
Then with a thrust
On her say
Started banging away
Chugging like a train
Or a screen door in a hurricane
Going full tilt
All the way to the hilt
A full frontal attack
With no holding back
From the drive
To feel more alive
Bringing the sensation
And stimulation
To a culmination
Finally overloading
And exploding
Achieving exultation and jubilation
Confirmation and validation
That occasionally positive happens,
Once in a while your average guy wins.

# From Behind
29 June 2009

From the moment we started
She was too kind hearted.
I mounted her doggy style
Which made me smile
And drool until she farted.

# Descend and Ascend Weekend
9 August 2009

Put me in a sling
Going out on a wing
Or upright standing
Make the flogger swing,
Do your thing
To make me sing.
Put me thru hell
And make me yell.
Help me release and fly
Until there is no more I.
There's a point above or below
Where there's no more ego.
Get me to converse
With the whole universe.
Remove the separations
That cause polarizations
Thru sensory stimulations.

# Three Husbands And A Wife
3 April 2011

As the labor pains finale
Alma was born in Castro Valley.
Abandoned, her mother's hopes were buried
And after being courted she remarried.
Alma grew up in the nitty-gritty
And wonder of San Francisco city.
As a flower child she thought it was trippy
To entertain the tourists as a hippie.
Her hair's natural curl
Made her an easily coifed girl;
But her natural hormone scheme
Dealt a fat blow to her self-esteem.
After hight school for more knowledge
She went to BYU college.
Following custom and norm
She lived in the Roman Ruins dorm.
Friends of friends stopped by
So she met a new guy.
Alma was his name,
Girl and boy called the same.
Date after date led
To them being wed.
She thought it would be cool
To attend beauty school.
His job was a data-entry clerk
And they met Mark thru his work.
Unfortunately, came the day
They divorced because he was gay.

Soon after in Utah
Mark married Alma.
Training looked like an income recipe
So they took classes in massage therapy.
She was a slow learner in a way
Because Mark also was gay.
By now Alma recognized it was true
She enjoyed sex with women too.
Then at a ren faire
She met George, a bear
Of a man who appreciated
Large women and they mated.
From the internet online
They found the Fat Sex gold mine.
At Panthea Con there grinned a
Mark and his Belinda.
Belinda's marriage lost its patina
And she changed her name to cyrena.
Alma's household now is three.
She, George and cyrena all agree
For some love is metered and measured,
For Alma love is available to be treasured.

# Crackerjack Boothlack

5 June 2011

Waiting, standing by the chair
I took off my coat and shirt,
Expecting the boothlack to get there,
And showing a little skin wouldn't hurt.
Finally he had things arranged to his taste
I stepped up, then sat back and relaxed
Knowing the job wouldn't be done in haste,
Getting my boots polished and waxed.
Not giving smudging a chance
As a preparatory chore
He rolled up my chaps and pants,
Then put my laces on the floor.
Next he licked the boot tongues clean
And with a rag he washed the soles.
So my boots were damp and pristine
Missing all the gunk from my strolls.
Indulging in his erotic niche
While ramping up his desire,
He sucked my boots as a fetish
And lit the shoe polish on fire.
With bare hands the wax was wrapped,
Spread on all surfaces in cahoots.
While the buffing cloth was snapped,
His cock got teased by my boots
Which made it stiffen and grow.
Then he whisked and polished
To make my boots shine and glow
Until all flaws were abolished.

Next my boots got relaced up.
With lambskin they were burnished,
So my reflection faced up.
My footwear had been refurnished.
He said "Watch your step, sir."
I realized my boots were done.
It was time for me to bestir
And exchange hugs for the fun.

# Drool Pool

1 May 2010

I drove to the bar
In my little car
Where I ran into my friend.
There was no need to pretend
The holes in his pants
Gave the whole bar a chance
To see he was there
Without underwear.
The game was pool
And my friend is no fool,
He got the other guy distracted
By the way he acted.
While aiming for a shot,
Believe it or not,
My friend posed in the right way
To put on a gratuitous display
Of his private family jewel.
You could call it dirty pool.